D1334762

Paddington

and the Tutti Frutti Rainbow

MICHAEL BOND

Paddington

and the Tutti Frutti Rainbow

illustrated by R.W. ALLEY

HarperCollins *Children's Books*

One day Mr Brown took Paddington and
all the family to the seaside for a treat.

Paddington sat in the front seat of the car
with Mr and Mrs Brown. Mrs Bird, who
looked after them, sat in the back with
Jonathan and Judy.

But when they got to the seaside it was raining hard and there was a gale blowing.

"Some treat!" said Mrs Bird, as she held on to her hat.

"Look!" cried Paddington. "That man's hair has blown away."

"Ssh!" hissed Judy. "His hair hasn't blown away. He's bald."

But Paddington pulled his duffle coat up
round his face. He didn't want his whiskers
to blow away.

"Let's go in this café," said Mrs Brown. "At least we'll be dry."

Paddington looked back at the sea. It was very rough.

"I think I'll put my arm bands on in case the tide comes in," he said.

As they sat down at a table, Mr Brown pointed to a picture on the wall. It showed an ice-cream called a Tutti Frutti Sundae.

"If you can say that, Paddington," he said, "I'll buy you one as a treat."

It was the biggest ice-cream Paddington had
ever seen and he tried several times to say it.

"Toothy Frutti… Futti Tooty… Flutti
Tutti…" But the more he tried the harder
it was.

"I think I may have a cornet instead, Mr Brown," he said sadly. "It isn't easy saying 'Tutti Frutti Sundae'."

Everybody laughed. And because in the end he had said it properly the girl brought him an extra large Sundae on a tray.

"I couldn't get any more ice-cream into the glass," she said.

"What a kind nurse!" exclaimed Paddington.

"She's not a nurse," said Judy. "She's
a waitress. Nurses look after people who
are ill."

"If Paddington eats all that," said Jonathan,
"he'll need a nurse."

Paddington gave Jonathan a hard stare.
"Bears are good at eating ice-cream," he said.

At that moment the sun came out. "I think it's going to be a nice day after all," said Mr Brown. "Look – there's a rainbow."

"Quick, Paddington," said Mrs Brown. "Look, before it goes away."

Paddington stared out of the window. He had
never seen a rainbow before.

"It looks just like my Tutti Frutti Sundae,"
he said.

"And it disappears nearly as quickly," said Mrs Bird, as the rainbow began to fade.

"You must make a wish," said Judy, "before the rainbow goes."

"Then we can play on the beach," said Jonathan.

"I wish," said Paddington happily, "I wish I could have a Tutti Frutti Rainbow every day of the week."